DETERMINED DETECTIVES

MERGER ON THE ORIENT EXPRESSWAY

by Mary Blount Christian

illustrated by Kathleen Collins Howell

E. P. Dutton   New York

to my mysterious friend,
Joan Lowery Nixon

Text copyright © 1986 by Mary Blount Christian
Illustrations copyright © 1986 by Kathleen Collins Howell

Library of Congress Cataloging in Publication Data
Christian, Mary Blount.
    Merger on the Orient Expressway.

(Determined Detectives)
    Summary: Fenton P. Smith and Gerald Grubbs, the
Determined Detectives, investigate a case of construction
bidding which has made Fenton's mother look like she's
being disloyal to her firm.
    [1. Mystery and detective stories] I. Howell,
Kathleen Collins, ill. II. Title. III. Series:
Christian, Mary Blount. Determined Detectives.
PZ7.C4528Me 1986 [Fic] 85-31109
ISBN 0-525-44231-6

Published in the United States by E. P. Dutton,
2 Park Avenue, New York, N.Y. 10016

Published simultaneously in Canada by
Fitzhenry & Whiteside Limited, Toronto

Editor: Julie Amper   Designer: Isabel Warren-Lynch
Printed in the U.S.A.   W   First Edition
10 9 8 7 6 5 4 3 2 1

7101139

CONTENTS

The Garage Sale

"Over there!" I shouted to Gerald as we were walking home after school. "See that sign? A garage sale! Maybe we can find a few more disguises cheap."

Gerald Grubbs and I are the sum total of a crackerjack investigative team called Determined Detectives. I, Fenton P. Smith, being the more imaginative of the two, am of course the main detective. Gerald is what you might call my Dr. Watson. We sometimes must go undercover to crack our cases, therefore the need for a variety of costumes. Unfortunately, we were without a case to solve at the moment. But it gave us a good opportunity to gather new disguises and practice our sleuthing skills.

"If they've got any cheap gold jewelry, I get dibs on that for our Egyptian report at school," I told Gerald. I figured I could bring a bunch of that junk and do my social studies report on all that gold stuff they found in King Tut's tomb. No need in making too big a deal; if you did that once, then the teachers were liable to expect you to make a big fuss over all their assignments.

Gerald shrugged. "Fine with me," he said. "I already know what I'm gonna do for my report."

"What?" I asked as I turned my pockets out, one after the other, looking for money.

"I'm not telling," Gerald said. "It's going to be a surprise."

That's not like Gerald, keeping secrets from me. "You're going to draw a picture of the pyramids, aren't you?"

"Nope," he said. "And don't ask because I'm not telling. It's going to be a big surprise."

I figured he'd eventually tell me. Gerald is not good at keeping secrets. "How much money do you have?" I asked.

Gerald rummaged through one pocket, then another, until he finally came up with two quarters, a dime, one nickel and four pennies. "I was planning on buying some bubble gum, though," he said.

"Bubble gum won't solve crimes; we need some new disguises!" I snapped. "Besides, I think I've got some gum at home. We can stop in, and I'll give you a piece." I managed to dig around and find a lint ball, two rubber bands, a quarter, a dime and two pennies. "Ummm," I mumbled. "Not much revenue of late. Whoever said crime doesn't pay was right."

Gerald sniggered. "Hey, that's funny, Fenton. Crime doesn't pay, heh." Gerald is a good audience.

We turned up the bush-edged driveway to the garage. A couple of women were standing around chattering while a bunch of little kids were giggling and screaming and chasing each other. They were running

2

around the card tables where bric-a-brac was spread out.

With my ability to see a scene quickly through the curious eyes of a detective, I also noted a cigar box of loose change and dollar bills there. Just as we got there, one of the little kids whammed into the table and sent money fluttering or rolling off in every direction.

One woman in slacks and a ponytail ran over to grab the kid by the arm and scream at him.

The other woman, whose miserable expression told me she was the garage owner, dropped to her knees and started grabbing up nickels and quarters that rolled in every direction.

Gerald and I knelt down to gather some of the way-ward money, and I caught sight of a little kid about to pocket a nickel that slid his way. "Ah hmmm," I said, clearing my throat and frowning at him.

He shrugged sheepishly and opened his fat little hand to drop the coin into my palm, alongside the rest of the money.

We handed the lady her change and helped her right her table. She smiled. "Thanks. Ten percent off anything you buy," she said gratefully.

"Great!" I said. "Do you have any authentic-looking jewelry? You know, Egyptian-looking stuff?" I asked. "I need some for a school project."

She looked around. "I did have some just a little while ago. But I see it's gone now."

Gerald and I went over to the rack of clothes. I thumbed through, looking for anything that might come in handy for disguises.

3

There were a couple of loud Hawaiian shirts—too noticeable for subtle detective work, a blue serge suit and—yeah, a couple of workman's coveralls that said A-Plus Service. If we rolled up the pants legs, they'd be just perfect.

I checked the prices. They were fifty cents each. With the ten percent discount, that would be forty-five cents apiece. That would leave us sixteen cents, I figured, doing quick computation in my head.

My eye fell on a fluffy pink feather boa. As embarrassing as it was, sometimes a good detective had to dress *really* different. That boa, fluffed up around the face and coupled with a fetching dress from one of our mothers' closets, would make a dandy disguise. I mean, who'd expect a he-man like one of us to show up in something like that? I could see the price tag dangling from it. Just fifteen cents. Perfect. I reached out to grab it and came face-to-face—or should I say, hand-to-hand—with someone else.

I tugged. The other hand tugged back. I pulled again. The other hand—so covered in freckles it looked like a speckled trout—pulled again. That hand looked distressingly familiar. I sniffed. Lavender perfume! It had to be!

I shoved back the clothes on the rack and this time really did come face-to-face with someone—the bane of my existence.

"Mae Donna Dockstadter!" I yelled.

There she stood, haughty as ever, those paprika-colored sausage curls sproinging all over her head like a bad case of Slinkies and her green cat-eyes glowering at me.

4

"Give me that boa!" she snarled. When she curled her lip, all her freckles melted into one big glob on her face.

I yanked back. "But I had it first!" I insisted. I could see the lady glancing over at us. "It's for my little sister!" I said, blushing.

"Don't be stupid!" Mae Donna yelled. "You don't have a sister."

I cringed as a couple of the women turned to look at me, their eyebrows raised into question marks.

"You can't kid me!" Mae Donna growled. "It's so you can play detective, isn't it?" Her voice was like a foghorn.

I shrank back against the clothes, wishing I could disappear. "We—we don't *play* detective," I argued. "We—we *detect!*"

"Whatever," she said, taking the moment of my misery to snatch the boa to herself. "Why don't you leave detective work to the experts—like me?" She glanced around quickly so her whorl of wienerlike curls tumbled into her face. "And like my father."

I let my hands fall to my sides, and she smiled triumphantly. Her freckles parted, lending themselves to a game of connect the dots, if only I'd had a pencil at that moment.

I, Fenton P. Smith, am usually the pillar of cool. And if it weren't for the fact that Mae Donna's father was a famous undercover agent, she'd never catch me off guard and defenseless like this. I often let her get the best of me in situations as a professional courtesy to him, a fellow detective.

I mean, I have to hand it to the guy. He has the best

6

cover of anybody I ever saw. People actually think he's a bug exterminator! If Mae Donna hadn't told me, I'd never have guessed his secret!

Gerald came up about that time. "Oh, hi, Mae Donna. Nice boa. Fenton, look what I found. And they're only two for a dime." He held up two engineer's caps. They'd be perfect with the coveralls.

"Great!" I said, whirling around to leave Mae Donna standing there with her stupid boa. "You can have the boa, Mae Donna," I said. "Feathers are the perfect complement for you." Before she could smile and say thank you, I added, "Feathers and turkeys just naturally seem to go together."

She hissed and came to stand behind us as we paid the lady for our items. Mae Donna was juggling the boa, her money and all the junk jewelry the woman had.

"Boy, Mae Donna," I said. "I bet you're going to use that jewelry for your social studies project. What a dumb idea. And lazy, too."

She jabbed her nose into the air. "A lot you know!" she snapped. "Humph!"

It was then that I noticed Mae Donna was carrying a cylinder-shaped bag with her. "What's in the bag, Mae Donna?" I asked. "Your *junior* magician's stuff?"

She raised her nose another couple of notches into the air. "I may be an amateur magician, Fenton, but I'm no junior anything! And what's in the bag is for me to know and you to find out!" she said. When I didn't act curious, she said, "Actually, though, I am branching out into the arts, if you *must* know." Her chin shot another three inches into the air. If it had started to rain, she'd have drowned!

Gerald and I paid for our stuff and left. But when we got to the end of the driveway, we scrunched behind some bushes. If there was anything that bothered me, it was Mae Donna having a secret from us. "Let's hide here," I whispered to my assistant. "Maybe we can find out what she's got in the bag."

I'd no sooner said that than Mae Donna, bathed in an overdose of lavender, came clumping down the drive. She was humming, "Tum tum te tum tum te tum" and doing a sort of hopping motion. She flung out her arms and whirled, flipping out one foot. Suddenly she lost her footing and came tumbling down on us, bush and all.

"The arts!" I shouted, struggling to my feet. "You said you were branching out into the arts! Of course! *Martial* arts! You are into karate!" For an instant I actually admired Mae Donna, but I caught myself and shook it off.

"You dum-dum!" she yelled, picking up herself, her bag and her pink feather boa and dusting herself off. "Not martial arts! *The* arts! That wasn't karate! That was *ballet!* That was *Swan Lake!*"

Gerald and I fell onto each other, rolling and laughing. "Swan! It looked like a goose to me!" I said, holding my sides.

"Leave it to someone as uncouth as you to say that!" she stormed. She stalked off, her head in the air, trailing her feather boa behind her.

"At least if she's caught up in learning how to dance, she won't be nosing into our detective business!" I assured Gerald.

We took our disguises to my house. Usually no one

8

is home this time of the afternoon. I let us in the back door with my own key.

"Mom!" I shrieked. "What are you doing here? What's the matter?"

"Arrrrrg!" she said. Her shoes were off, and her stocking feet were propped up on the stool. She was wearing an ice pack on her forehead and a worried look.

"I just can't believe this is happening to me! This is the fourth time I've placed a bid on a construction job only to be beaten out by just a couple of dollars. And it's always that same firm."

I shrugged sympathetically as I shoved Gerald toward my room. "Gee, that's too bad, Mom," I said. "But I guess that happens sometimes, huh?"

"Once, maybe," she said. "Perhaps twice. But four times? Impossible. How it could happen four times is a mystery to me!"

Gerald and I stopped dead in our tracks. We grinned at each other and poked our heads back into the room to be sure we heard right.

I could feel my insides tingling. I took a deep breath. "Did you say *mystery?*"

Mystery Begins
at Home

I scooted back into the room to sit on the stool. Mom shifted her feet over to make room for me. Gerald came in and plopped on the other chair. We leaned forward, waiting expectantly for her to fill us in on the details.

"Well?" I said at last when she failed to continue. "Maybe it'll help if you talk about it. We're all ears, Mom."

"Arrrrrg!" she said once more. "That's all there is to it! I told you everything. I study the proposals, check all the prices our subcontractors will give us, then type up the bid and seal it and turn it in. But every time, Stern Construction undercuts my bid by a few dollars. Not a hundred, not a thousand. Just a few dollars! And to add insult to injury, my typewriter's acting up." She moaned miserably. "I need a vacation!"

I glanced at Gerald and raised my eyebrows slightly as a signal. I figured we'd just found our next case. He nodded his agreement.

"Could the bids have been steamed open, then resealed?" I asked.

"No," Mom said. "There is no way Stern or anybody else could get a look at my bids. I keep them in my possession at all times! And that isn't the worst! Mine are the *only* bids this is happening to. I think my boss suspects me of foul play! Working with that balky typewriter is bad enough. Having your boss suspicious of you is horrid." She shifted the ice pack on her head. "I should never have told him about that test I took."

Mom takes all those dumb magazine tests. You know the kind—"How To Tell If Your Kids Are Going To Grow Up To Be President," "Should You Be An Astronaut?" and this last one, the one she must be talking about, "How Honest Are You?"

It asked stupid questions like, "If your best friend asks you what you think of her unflattering dress, would you (1) tell her she looks wonderful, (2) say something vague like 'I can just see this with a matching handbag' or (3) tell her how ugly it is." Mom, being the kind person she is, answered she'd rave about the dress and flunked the test. She's been in a funk ever since.

"Maybe there is a computer whiz at Stern who breaks into your system and reads your bids," I suggested. I'd read about people doing that sort of thing.

"Arrrrrg!" Mom said again, rolling her eyes at me. "I can't use that computer. I am just not up to those modern electronic monsters yet. I still use my typewriter." She shrugged. "Sorry."

"Maybe somebody is reading your carbons," Gerald suggested. It sounded reasonable to me.

"I always shred my carbons—and my worksheets," Mom said. "I'm taking a few days off, boys. Maybe when I go back—if I *can* go back, that is—everything

12

will be okay." She sat bolt upright in the chair and threw the ice pack aside. "I think I'll bake an eggplant and squash casserole. Then maybe I'll clean out that hall closet and—"

I wrinkled my nose at the thought of eggplant and squash casserole—gross. Mom cooks the dopiest things to get over depression. She firmly believes that food is the solution to every problem. But the really bad sign was cleaning the hall closet. First thing you know, she'll be on my case to clean my room, maybe even my closet! I pride myself in the fact that it is a regular museum to my childhood. I haven't thrown anything away since I was five years old. I signaled Gerald to get us out of there in a hurry.

"I gotta get home," Gerald said, picking up on my signal.

I leaped up. "I'll walk you to the corner," I volunteered. Maybe by the time I got back, Mom would be squishing up the eggplant for her icky casserole, and she wouldn't be thinking about the cleaning part.

"I'm desperate, Gerald," I said when we were outside. "We gotta clear my mom's name and get her back to work or she'll be baking asparagus mousse next and having us polish the doorknobs!"

I narrowed my eyes and looked up and down the street before continuing. "We gotta solve this mystery. Preferably," I added, "without the questionable help of that rotten old Mae Donna Dockstadter!"

Not a Clue
to Their Names

"Does anybody want your job?" I asked Mom at supper that night. "I mean, might somebody at work be trying to make you look bad so they can get your job?" I chewed slowly. I knew if my plate was emptied too fast she'd take that as a sign I needed more of her eggplant and squash casserole. It tasted like papier-mâché.

"Certainly not!" Mom said, dishing another tablespoon of it on my plate anyway. "Besides, almost everyone there has a higher paying job than I do." She paused, a finger to her lips. "Well, there is Harry Marple; he worked for Stern until about a year ago. Maybe—" She shook her head vigorously. "No, that's silly! Harry thinks Mr. Stern is a jerk. He wouldn't do anything to help him. And I suspect that Mr. Melrose will make him a junior partner soon anyway. He's quite good!"

Mom blushed slightly. "Although Mr. Melrose does give me the more *important* jobs, I must say."

Dad made a face and swallowed a bite of casserole. "It's probably just some strange coincidence. Maybe

14

you could make the estimate, then cut off five or ten dollars just as a safeguard, dear."

Mom sighed and dipped the spoon into the casserole. I scooted my plate away from her reach, so she dropped that glob of horrible stuff into Dad's plate. He turned a shade of green and moaned. I knew I had to get this case cracked if our stomachs were going to survive.

She snuffled. "Everybody at work thinks I've sold out to the enemy." Her lip trembled. "I can just tell from the funny way they look at me and stop whispering when I come near. And my b-b-boss even suggested I take some time off." She turned away and blew her nose. When she turned back to us, her eyes were all misty. "He just wants me out of there because we have that bid coming up. He must think I'm the one who's selling out to the other firm. Why else would he send me home?"

"Now, dear," my father said, patting her hand gently. "This is just his way of trying to help. You said yourself that you were so upset you kept mixing up your papers and dropping things and that your typewriter was broken. He just wants you back fresh and happy when things are better."

As little as I relished the idea of Mom staying home with me, it was perfect that Mom was going to take a few days off. That was a good opportunity for Gerald and me to do some detective work. A fellow doesn't want to do dangerous work like going undercover if his mother is going to be hanging around worrying or maybe even recognizing him and ruining everything.

After supper I gathered my disguise for the next day and stuffed it in my book satchel. Then I looked around

15

for something I could do for my social studies project. I rummaged through my closet—at least the top couple of layers of it.

I found an old Monopoly set, a couple of plastic cowboys and Indians, a dinosaur and an old teddy bear with only one button eye. The ribbon around his neck was in shreds. Ummm. That gave me an idea. If I got a bunch of first-aid gauze, and I wrapped it around and around—a mummy! That's what I'd do for my social studies project. I'd make a mummy.

Satisfied that I had at least one problem solved, I went to bed. I needed plenty of sleep if I was going to solve the other problem—clearing Mom's good name by finding out just how the bids could have been tampered with, or if all of this was really just a weird coincidence.

I decided we should ride our bikes to school the next day, then pedal on over to Strident Construction, mom's company. The office is about three miles away on the expressway to the little town of Orient.

I also instructed my assistant to bring his A-Plus Service coveralls and his engineer's cap. I had an idea about how we could snoop around in there without arousing suspicion.

We decided to eat our lunches outside on the school campus. That way we could make our plans away from the prying eyes and ears of the other kids, especially that weird, snoopy old Mae Donna Dockstadter.

"I'll trade you a whole cup of leftover eggplant and squash casserole for just half of that peanut butter and jelly sandwich," I said, eyeing Gerald's Spiderman lunchbox full of goodies.

"No thanks," Gerald said. "So how are we going to go undercover at Strident Construction?"

"I'll throw in my apple and three carrot sticks," I said. "With our A-Plus Service uniforms. Remember? Mom said her typewriter was broken."

"I wouldn't take your eggplant and squash casserole if you threw in your piece of sponge cake with walnut frosting," Gerald said. He licked his lips, giving me added hope. "So what has your mother's typewriter and our uniforms got to do with getting us into Strident Construction without being caught?" he asked.

Sometimes I wondered why I bother trying to train Gerald as my assistant. I mean, he can be so dense! "My eggplant and squash casserole, four carrot sticks, my sponge cake with walnut frosting and two sticks of bubble gum," I said. "We are going to go undercover as typewriter repairmen, of course!" I waved the sponge cake close to his nose.

Gerald sniffed once, twice. I knew I had him then. He shoved his peanut butter and jelly sandwich toward me and snatched at the cake. "All of it, Gerald!" I insisted. "Unless you eat the eggplant and squash casserole, too, the deal's off!"

He shrugged and picked up the plastic spoon, digging into the cup of casserole. "But we don't know anything about repairing typewriters. How are we going to fool the people at her office?"

"They don't know anything about repairing typewriters either, or they'd do it themselves," I reminded him. I pulled out my toolbox filled with screwdrivers, pliers, a hammer and wrenches. "So how hard can it be to fix?" I asked. "We'll just sort of fool around with some of the tools, making fixing noises, then squirt a little oil on it. That always works for my dad when the garage door is stuck. That, and a good swift kick, that is."

I glanced at my wristwatch. "We still got a few minutes before the bell rings. Let's review what we know about this case, okay?"

Gerald bit into the sponge cake and made a few "mmmmmm" noises, nodding okay.

My stomach growled accusingly. I polished off the last bite of peanut butter and jelly sandwich, then pulled out my case notebook. "Okay," I said, scanning my hasty notes. "Mom says that four times she has been underbid by the same company, Stern Construction, by just a couple of dollars."

"Yeah," Gerald added, licking some of the walnut icing off his lip, "and she says she's the only one in her company that this is happening to."

"Right," I said.

"And she said that she was positive the sealed bids weren't steamed open, read and resealed. She said they never left her possession until they were turned in to the bid committee," Gerald added.

I nodded, pleased that my assistant had been paying attention for a change. "And I've been to one of those bid openings with her," I said. "Everybody gets into this one room—the bidders and the bid committee. They all watch right there while somebody opens the bids and reads them out loud."

"What about her carbons?" a foghorn voice from behind the bush asked.

I sniffed. Lavender perfume! "Mae Donna Dockstadter, bug off!" I yelled.

She stepped out. "Don't say *bug* to me!" she snarled.

To tell the truth, I hadn't even thought about that. I guess she would be a little sensitive about her father's cover as a bug exterminator. If it weren't for professional courtesy to her father, I wouldn't be above deliberately mentioning bugs around her—especially now that I know it *bugs* her. "How long have you been spying on us?" I demanded.

She grinned from ear to ear. "I *knew* you didn't know it! Some detective! I asked, what about your mother's carbons? I mean, it would certainly be simple for someone to just hold those carbons to the light and read them, don't you think?"

I folded my arms defensively. "We've already eliminated the carbons as the problem, Miss Snoop!" I growled. "She puts them through the shredder. Why don't you take your twinkle toes somewhere else and practice your ballet or karate or whatever you are doing? This is *our* case."

Mae Donna stuck her nose into the air. Her kinky old red curls looked as if they'd been combed with an egg beater. "It certainly sounds to me as if you could use some *expert* help. You two heroes aren't coming up with the solution on your own! And typewriter repairmen? Ha! That's a stupid disguise if I ever heard one."

I could feel my ears growing warm. They were probably as red as her hair. "Oh, yeah?" I said, glaring at her. "And just what would *you* be to get into the office without being noticed?" The minute I'd said that I was sorry. I hoped I hadn't given her any crazy ideas.

Her little green pig-eyes glistened with an idea. Her grin spread from one freckle-spotted ear to the other. "Oh, whatever," she said, shrugging. But I could tell that she had a plan in that weaselly mind of hers.

The bell rang, calling us back inside. Mae Donna whirled around and traipsed toward the building, her nose at a forty-five-degree angle to the ground.

I could feel sweat beads over my lip and eyebrows as I hastily gathered my tools back into the case and picked up the lunch litter, such as it was. "Now I'm really worried," I confided in my assistant. "We have enough on our hands just clearing Mom. Now we've got to worry about what that dumb old Mae Donna will do."

"She's probably just bluffing," Gerald said. "Don't worry. And by the way, Fenton, I don't see what you have against your mother's eggplant and squash casserole. It's not half-bad!"

It figured; Gerald must have an iron stomach. He would be really crazy about her turnip and artichoke soufflé! But he wasn't my main concern right then.

I wondered, just how much of our conversation had Mae Donna heard. Did she know the name of my mother's construction firm? I hoped not. But somehow I wouldn't put it past Mae Donna to horn in on our investigation somehow. She could blow the whole thing!

Too Many Detectives

After school, Gerald and I slipped into the rest room and changed into our A-Plus Service coveralls, our false noses and moustaches, and our engineer's caps.

I opened the door a crack and looked up and down the hall. Nobody in sight. Maybe dumb old Mae Donna had left for another ballet lesson and forgotten all about us. By now she was probably stepping all over some poor guy's toes.

The teachers were in a faculty meeting in the auditorium, so we didn't have to worry about running into any of them. "Be on the lookout for Mae Donna, just in case," I warned my assistant.

When we were sure the coast was clear, we slipped out to our bicycles, then pedaled as fast as we could down the Orient Expressway. We parked our bikes outside the building where Mom worked and went in.

"Your company said it couldn't send anyone to fix the typewriter until next week," the secretary said. She eyed us suspiciously.

I twirled my false moustache. "So why question your

good fortune?" I asked. "We got ahead of schedule."

"So why does it take two people to fix one typewriter?" she asked. "We are not paying two people!"

"He's in training," I said. "He's free."

She pointed us toward the door to the offices. "In there," she said.

Gerald sniffled. He always does that when he gets scared. That didn't exactly raise my confidence. I nodded with as much assurance as I could, and walked in. Gerald followed. It was one big room with lots of partitions to make lots of little rooms.

A chalkboard at the front had the names of the employees. I wrote them down. Cassandra Smith (my mom), Sam Bradford (junior architect), Nancy Melrose (another junior architect and the boss's daughter), Jeffrey Melrose (the president), and Harry Marple (the other project manager, although he isn't as important as my mom). But she's been with the company nine years, and Harry's only been with it for a year.

He's the one who used to work for Stern Construction, the competition just down the street (the one that keeps beating out my mom on the bids).

The chalkboard had little In and Out columns. By my mom's name, it said Day Off. Harry and Nancy showed they were on coffee breaks. Melrose was out to lunch, although it was nearly four o'clock now—so much for being the boss. And Sam was marked as On Assignment. Back Tomorrow. That left the whole back office empty, so we could snoop freely.

There were lots of little alcoves in the room. Each was piled high with jumbles of papers and folders. You

24

could turn this way and that. I felt as if I should find a piece of cheese at the end of the maze.

Then I saw my mom's name on the side of one of the doors: Cassandra Smith, Project Manager. It looked pretty impressive. I'm not saying that just because she's my mom. It's true. I poked my head into one of the offices and was surprised to see somebody down on his hands and knees under the desk. "Oh!" I yelled, startled.

Whump! The guy bumped his head, trying to get out from under the desk. He rose, rubbing his head, which was covered with bushy red curls.

"Mr. Dockstadter!" I said.

He squinted at me, as if trying to recall who I was or where he'd seen me before.

I pulled off the false nose a minute. "It's me!" I whispered. I swallowed my pride and tried not to choke on the words. "You know, Mae Donna's friend. Gosh, if I'd known *you* were on the case, I wouldn't have been so worried."

"Case? Oh, uh yes, Finnegan," he said.

"Fenton," I corrected. "Yessir, it is really comforting, knowing that you are here taking care of the problem. Have you found anything yet?"

"No," Mr. Dockstadter said. "But I'm not surprised. I come by every six months or so just to be sure."

"Really? And they don't suspect a thing?"

"Suspect? Well, Frederick—"

"Fenton," I said. Important detectives must have a lot on their minds. He probably saves all his thinking for his cases. "Do you have any more advice for me, sir?" I asked. "I always appreciate any advice you give me, you know."

"Oh, yes, Faxton," he said. "You plan to be a bug man, don't you?"

I chuckled. Always the undercover man. What an act! "Yes, sir," I said, winking to let him know I understood perfectly. "Any suggestions?"

He scratched his head, thinking. "Always do exactly what your client expects of you. Always check the refuse, Fendly. Not everyone thinks of that. But it's important to check the refuse." He straightened his shoulders proudly.

I nodded. "Yessir, do what's expected and check the refuse. I'll remember that, sir. Well, I guess I'd better let you get back to work. Got to stop the bugger in his tracks, right?"

He crawled back under the desk, and I scooted into Mom's office. Wow, I figured if I could solve the case before Mr. Dockstadter, what a deal that would be. Maybe he'd let me assist him sometimes!

I joined Gerald in Mom's office, where he was poking and prying through papers. "Anything?" I asked. But he hadn't seen anything that even looked like a clue.

I heard the secretary's heels clicking toward us, so Gerald and I hovered over the typewriter. I carefully watched out of the corner of my eye. She had somebody with her, somebody from Wonder Woman Temporary Help, she said.

This freckly person tottered in on wobbly high heels. She was wearing a large floppy hat pulled down over her eyes, a dress that looked as if it had come from somebody's attic and a pink feather boa—most inappropriate for office attire.

As she wobbled past us, I got a distinct whiff of lavender perfume. Mae Donna Dockstadter!

"The files are here, the cabinets there," the secretary said. "Use your logic to file, and you'll be just fine." She paused to peer suspiciously at us once more before clicking off to her desk in the foyer.

Mae Donna Dockstadter use her logic? Ha! That was like telling an amoeba to think!

When the secretary was out of sight, I stalked over to Mae Donna. "What do you think you are doing here, horning in on *our* case?" I stormed.

Mae Donna grabbed a file marked *Morris Mansion* and stuck it in the *R* drawer. "It is not just *your* case," she said, sneering so her freckles kind of globbed into one. "I bet I solve it before you do!"

"You will not!" I argued. "Furthermore, your father is here working on the case. How many detectives do you think one case takes?"

Her green eyes widened. "My father? Here?" She pulled her floppy hat down further over her face. She hovered over the filing cabinet, her freckled nose buried in a file.

For one tiny second, I could almost sympathize with dumb old Mae Donna. I mean, I understood what pressure a parent hanging around could put you under. I just felt lucky that my own mom was not here, even though at this very minute she was probably at home, dreaming up jobs for me to do—like clean all the fuzz balls from under my bed and straighten up my toys and unreasonable stuff like that.

"And besides, what are you doing putting *Morris Mansion* under *R*?" I asked.

She clicked her tongue against her teeth and rolled her eyes as if she thought I were the dumbest kid in the world. "Be logical!" she insisted. "What is a mansion if it isn't a castle? And who owns castles? Kings and queens, that's who. And what are kings and queens? They are royalty, of course! And *royalty* begins with *r*. Honestly, Fenton. Sometimes I wonder about you!"

I threw up my hands in surrender and hustled back to the typewriter, where Gerald had spread out the tools.

Mr. Dockstadter had advised me, always do what your clients expect. And this client expected the typewriter to be repaired. I knew I had better do something to the typewriter. That secretary was going to come checking any minute again. First, I unsnapped the ribbon cassette, then I turned the typewriter over and found some screws. I loosened the screws, and the whole top just popped right off. This was going to be a snap.

I saw a little brass screw holding down a spring, which was attached to a thin rod. I unscrewed it.

Sproing! The spring flew into the air about four feet and landed in an ivy plant. The rod clinked to the desk. A couple of little wires rolled from the typewriter and tumbled to the floor.

"Look busy," I whispered.

To my dismay, Gerald grabbed the ribbon cassette and pulled. It came whirring out in a long inky string, tangling and smudging everything, including us. I snatched the cassette and jammed it and the jumble of ribbon into the toolbox as I heard the secretary's *click, click, click*ing down the hall toward us.

She stuck her head into the little office. "It'll be closing time soon," she said. "Are you almost through?"

I looked at the pieces of typewriter spread across the desk. There must have been a jillion of them. Who'd have thought that there'd be so many parts in one little typewriter? "Er, this may be more serious than I first thought. This typewriter is really falling apart!"

"Then you'll just have to come back tomorrow!" she said. She whirled on her heels and stalked off to the other room. She looked like a big Mae Donna. Acted like her, too.

"Look at all this stuff!" Gerald moaned. He sniffled. "What are we going to do?"

"Gerald, I can't be worried about little details like that!" I wailed. "I've got a case to solve! Now, quick, while she's out in the foyer, let's look around some." I figured even if we didn't find any clues, I might be able to look at one of the other typewriters and see just how it was put together. It's really dumb of those typewriter companies not to number the parts the way they do on model kits.

We checked the other offices. There were no more typewriters. All the others used computers. Could Mom's typewriter have anything to do with the information leak? How?

I heard the secretary coming back again, *click, click, click.* If she saw all these parts again! . . . I swept them all—ribbon, nuts, bolts, springs and all—into my toolbox and snapped it shut.

"I'll have to come back tomorrow with some parts," I said, smiling at her from under my moustache.

"Fine," she said, kind of preoccupied. "Everybody out!" she called loud enough so Mae Donna would get the message, too. I had the feeling this woman wasn't about to work a second longer than she had to. That indicated a certain lack of company loyalty and dedication to this detective. I made a mental note to add her to my list of suspects. It now included everybody who worked there except Mom. This wasn't going to be an easy one.

Closing in Fast!

Well, I was right about one thing. Mom had whipped up her horrible mushroom–rutabaga–collard-green pie. I think she must get all her recipes from Lucrezia Borgia.

I could smell it baking when I got home. I went straight to the den. There was no need in letting her see me. She would just start handing out jobs for me to do. Hang up my clothes. Make up my bed. Get my roller skates out of the middle of the hall. Having a mother home could be the pits!

I wanted to see just how the typewriter was put together. I figured if I sketched a diagram of it, matched its parts to the ones in my toolbox, maybe I could get Mom's office typewriter together again with no one (especially Mom) the wiser for it. I tapped on the keys a little. *Now is the time for all good detectives to come to the aid of their mothers. Now is the time* . . . Everything worked fine on this typewriter. Now if I could just duplicate the inner workings on the typewriter at work.

Next problem, my social studies project. "Mom?" I

called. "Did you get me a whole bunch of gauze today?"

She came in with about four boxes of it. "I told the druggist what you needed it for. He said since it wasn't for first-aid purposes anyway, he'd just give you these damaged boxes. See? There's a little bit of ink on them so they couldn't possibly be used for bandages."

I thanked her and made a mental note to thank the druggist, too. Then I went to my room to wrap the teddy bear like a mummy. I figured Mae Donna would bring her box of fake gold jewelry and report on the Egyptian riches. But what about Gerald? I hoped that Gerald hadn't decided to do a mummy, too. That wouldn't look good to the teacher if the two of us had the exact same report. She might think Gerald copied me. Or worse! She might think *I* copied *Gerald.* He still hadn't given me even a hint.

I crossed the teddy bear's paws like the mummies I'd seen in pictures. Then I started wrapping the gauze around and around. The ink spots looked pretty gunky, but maybe I could pretend that the cloth was rotten or something.

It's funny how the little ink patterns on the cloth had sort of soaked through layer after layer. I held the gauze up to the light. Was this going to look too dopey on a mummy? I squinted at the little spots on the gauze. Then it hit me! I ran into the den and yanked the ribbon cassette from the typewriter. I pulled on the ribbon and held it up to the light. There it was, as plain as if it were on the paper itself. *Now is the time for all good detectives to come to the aid of their mothers.*

I ran back to my room and got the jumble of ribbon from my toolbox. My heart sank. It was blank. Of

course! The only way to keep Mom from suspecting anything would be to replace the cassette that was taken out. Naturally this one would be blank!

"Mom!" I yelled, running through the house and waving the ribbon from the den typewriter. "Mom!" I ran into the kitchen. "Mo—*ulp!*"

She shoved a spoonful of mushroom–rutabaga–collard-green pie into my mouth. "How is that?" she asked.

It tasted like wet concrete. "Uh, *ulp*. Uh, interesting," I said. "Interesting. But Mom, I know how your secret bids weren't really secrets! Look!" I held the ribbon up for her to read.

"Now is the time for all good detectives to come to the aid of their mothers," she read. "That's sweet, dear. I appreciate your support in my hour of distress."

"Don't you see, Mom?" I said, trying not to show my exasperation. "Somebody's been reading your *ribbons!*"

She stood there, her mouth hanging open. "Why, that's—that's incredible! Fenton, you are so clever! Have you ever considered becoming a detective when you grow up? I'll go in there tomorrow and just tell Mr. Melrose!" she said, giving me a hug as if I were a little kid.

"No, Mom!" I said. "I mean, that's only the *how!* That isn't the *why* or, more important, the *who*. It could even be Mr. Melrose; we won't know until we bait the trap."

Mom stood there, the stirring spoon still held in midair, still dripping mushroom–rutabaga–collard-green pie. "Bait the trap? Fenton, what are you talking about?"

"Mom," I explained slowly. "You are going to go back to work as if you don't suspect a thing. You are going to let everybody there know about the new bid you are making. Then we'll just see who takes the bait —or the ribbon."

Mom giggled. "Why do I feel as if I'm in a James Bond movie? How exciting!"

"Uh, just one thing, Mom," I said. "You might want to take the family typewriter to work with you."

She raised an eyebrow questioningly.

"Call it a hunch," I said. "I haven't been wrong so far, have I?"

I figured if I was right, by this time tomorrow we'd have our thief, and the Smiths would be eating decent food again. And *this* Smith won't be searching out fuzz balls under his bed!

I finished wrapping the teddy bear for my project, although it wasn't due until the day after tomorrow because of a half-day off (teacher in-service training) in the afternoon. Fenton P. Smith is not a procrastinator! Besides, I wanted to be sure I had saved enough time for our case.

The plan was for Mom to work all morning on her fake bid, then to make up some excuse to leave the office for the afternoon. That would leave the thief some time to take the ribbon, and it would get Mom out of the way so Gerald and I could return in our disguises without Mom catching on. I only hoped that Mae Donna Dockstadter had a more pressing engagement.

Four Red Herrings

On the way to Mom's office the next day, I pumped Gerald about his project. "I bet you are going to bring a bunch of figs and raisins and stuff and talk about what the Egyptians ate, aren't you?"

"Nope!" Gerald said. He grinned wide and mysteriously.

"I bet you are going to bring a jar of water and talk about the Nile River," I guessed.

"Nope," he said. "You'll see."

We waited until we saw Mom leave, then we went in.

"It's about time!" the secretary said, glaring at us. "Where did you have to send for those parts? Alaska?"

I shrugged. "Is there a larger empty office where we can work?" I asked. "My assistant gets claustrophobia in small places."

Gerald glared at me. "Why do *I* always have to seem like the weird one?" he asked when she had left us.

"It was the best excuse I could think of to get out of Mom's office and give the thief a free hand," I said.

Besides, I was doing the talking. Did he really think I'd say something like that about myself? I figured we could take the typewriter into the file room and still have a clear view of Mom's office.

To my dismay, Mae Donna was already there, filing in her inscrutable system of "logic."

"Nothing so far," she whispered in her foghorn voice.

"How did you know we were coming back today?" I asked. "Have you been spying on us again?"

She shrugged. "Whatever."

I took out my diagram and started sticking parts back into the typewriter, all the time keeping one eye on Mom's office.

People were in and out of there all afternoon. There was Nancy, but I dismissed her as a suspect because she was the boss's daughter, and she had a lot more to gain if the business was profitable and in her father's hands.

Then there was Harry, a good suspect because maybe he wanted to be my mom—that is, the *top* project manager. Besides, he had worked for the Stern Construction firm, the one that was benefiting from the information. Maybe he had never quit working for Stern. Maybe now he was a spy.

The only other people in and out of Mom's office were the secretary, who kept glaring at us, and Marvin, the janitor, who tidied up and emptied the wastebaskets into his great big wastebin on wheels. I began to panic. What if *nobody* took our bait?

I slipped into the office and looked. The ribbon was still in the typewriter. I looked closer. This ribbon hadn't been typed on. It was brand new, although Mom had worked all morning on the typewriter. Somebody had switched ribbons. But where was the ribbon?

I rushed back to Gerald and Mae Donna. "The ribbon's gone!" I said. "People have taken things into the office all day. But the only thing that has gone out was trash! Marvin took the trash!"

"That's it!" I said. "That's what Mr. Dockstadter was talking about! He said, check the refuse! The trash basket! The ribbon is in the trash bin. Marvin is the one! He's probably tired of cleaning up after everybody here and wants to really *clean up* in the white-collar espionage game!"

Gerald looked at me with that I-don't-get-it look, so I tried again. "White-collar espionage. That's spying in the business world. And cleaning up—I mean he's making money by selling secrets."

We could still see the janitor. He was making his way into each office, dumping the trash into his big barrel on wheels.

We watched until he pushed past the secretary, nodding and whistling. He pushed the barrel right out the door. The secretary scooted from her desk and was bending over some shelves with stacks of folders on them. The three of us slipped past her and followed the janitor. He dumped the trash into a big refuse container out back.

When he went back in, we all ran over and rummaged through the papers he'd thrown in. There was the ribbon. Marvin hadn't done anything with it. He didn't even try to be careful with it. He acted as if he didn't care about the ribbon—or maybe he didn't *know*

about it. This was going to take all my detective cunning, all my skills.

"That means that one of them went into the office, stuck a new ribbon cassette into the typewriter, threw the used one into the trash basket, knowing that Marvin would pick it up and throw it back here. All we have to do is wait to see who shows up to retrieve it."

We skulked into the shadows of the alley and waited. After a while, Harry came out. He looked both ways. Then he pulled out a cigarette and lit it. When he had finished it, he went back in. He hadn't come near the container. Had he seen us?

"Mom's boss won't let anybody smoke in the office," I whispered. "I guess Harry just wanted to sneak a smoke." My brain snapped into high gear. "Or maybe that is a signal to somebody!"

Nancy Melrose came out. She rubbed her arms as if she were chilly, and stood in the sunshine. She looked up and down the alley, then walked over to the trash bin. I thought, this is it! The boss's daughter is going to get the ribbon!

But she only blew one more bubble, then threw her gum into the trash bin. She went back inside.

No sooner had the door closed than it opened again. Sam Bradford stepped out into the sunlit alley. He reached into the air, then stooped to touch his toes. He bent his arm. making a muscle, and puffed out his chest. I nearly giggled out loud. He was watching his shadow, admiring it! He went back inside. Could *that* have been a signal? I wondered.

Finally Jeffrey Melrose himself came outside. Could

the culprit be the boss? What would his motive be? Why would *he* want to make his company go bankrupt? As we quietly watched, he shaded his eyes with his hands and looked to his left and right, then he took quick steps toward the trash bin. He reached into his pocket and pulled out a candy bar. He gobbled it down, then threw the wrappings into the trash bin. Mom had often said that he was on a diet. He probably didn't want anyone to know he was cheating on it.

When he had gone in, Harry Marple came out again. He snacked on a cupcake, then threw the wrapping into the trash bin. All of them had been near the container with the ribbon, but nobody made any moves to take it out. I was getting tired of staying all cramped up like that.

Finally a car pulled to the end of the driveway. It honked twice and paused. Then it honked once. We got down behind some boxes and couldn't see anything. But I could hear something. *Click, click, click,* heels tapped against the concrete alley. I jotted down the license plate of the car I had observed. It was a personalized plate: STERN ONE. Stern—the name of the company that was always underbidding Mom. And I bet that ONE was the big boss himself.

Click, click, click. The steps came close to the container, and we huddled low. We could hear someone rummaging through the trash. Then *click, click, click,* the steps moved toward the car.

"Don't let him get that," I said, stepping from the shadows. "Stop!" I said. "Stop!"

Mae Donna was a lot closer to them. But she wasn't

doing anything but staring wide-eyed. Her green eyes looked like side-by-side bowls of lime Jell-O. I had to do something. I started to hum that tune she said was *Swan Lake.* "Tum tum te tum tum te tum." Mae Donna caught the idea, and on the last "tum" she whirled around and kicked the ribbon right out of the secretary's hands. There's something to be said for clumsiness at times.

All our yelling had attracted a crowd. "What's going on here?" Mr. Melrose demanded. "Stern! What are you doing back here in our alley? And Martha!" he said, looking at the secretary.

"This is how those bids were undercut," I said.

"Martha here would sneak out the cassette ribbons to Stern. And he could bid just a few dollars under," Mae Donna interrupted.

I glared at her, and she shot her nose into the air with a loud "Humph!"

"Mrs. Smith is innocent," I said.

"Well, of course she is!" Mr. Melrose said. "She is a good worker. I never suspected her—not really. She was just such a nervous wreck from all this, that I was afraid she would quit work. And she's the best worker I have. I couldn't stand it if she quit!"

I shuddered at the thought. I couldn't stand it, either. I was relieved to hear that she was never really a suspect. And I was glad to hear from Melrose that he was going to fire his secretary.

"It was really a simple case, once the method was discovered, wasn't it?" I said to Gerald and Mae Donna on our way home. "Mr. Stern didn't really want Stri-

42

dent Construction out of business. He only wanted the two companies to merge—Stern and Strident Construction. His was actually the smaller and weaker of the two companies."

"But if he could momentarily make Strident seem weak and unprofitable, he figured maybe the weak could swallow up the profitable," Mae Donna interrupted. "He figured if he could weaken the company enough, keep it from making any money for a while, he'd be able to get Mr. Melrose to accept his offer to merge."

I gave Mae Donna a lengthy glare. What a show-off! I felt pretty good that we had cracked this case (and that I had only one small typewriter piece leftover after putting it back together).

I had renewed admiration for Mr. Dockstadter, too. His idea about looking in the refuse was brilliant. When I stopped by his house to thank him for his help, he acted as if he didn't even understand what I was talking about. He is one cool detective. I can only hope that Gerald and I will be half that good.

Mom was really happy that night. She must have been. We had my favorites for dinner—spaghetti and meatballs with applesauce and even some strawberry ice cream for dessert. Thank goodness!

"I'm going to make a real effort to work on the computer from now on," Mom said at dinner.

"You'll love it!" Dad said. "Just give yourself a couple of days, and you'll get the hang of it. I'm glad you decided to join the twentieth century."

"Well," Mom said. "It wasn't hard to decide after

typing on my old typewriter. It's the weirdest thing. I typed *Now is the time . . .* and it came out *blysfitglmpt.* Can you imagine?"

I blushed; I could imagine. At least Mom was dealing with the problem in a positive way.

I took my mummy to school the next day. I carried him in a sack and wouldn't show Gerald because he was still being so secretive about his social studies project.

Mae Donna came in, her head in the air and her sausage curls bouncing around like rusty bedsprings in a high wind. She had used the junk jewelry from the garage sale for her social studies project, just as I had deduced. But she had made a bigger-than-life papier-mâché head of Cleopatra and painted it gold and used all the jewelry. What a show-off!

Several of us did mummies, so I guess that wasn't too original an idea, after all. But talk about original ideas! Gerald really took the prize (and a week's worth of detention).

When it was his turn to give his report, he pulled out a little box of sand and an electric fan.

"My report," he said, "is on the desert storms." And he turned on the fan!